To Ray & Anne Louise – from
The people who live in
the North.

love

Dale

Random House · Toronto

CROW and WEASEL

by Barry Lopez

Illustrations by Tom Pohrt

Author's Note

Crow and Weasel, set in myth time and written with respect for Native
American values and oral tradition, is a work of fiction. It does not
derive, as far as I know, from any indigenous North American tradition.

Illustrator's Note

Items of material culture in the drawings, including clothing, saddles,
and parfleches are derived from northern Plains Native American de-
signs. The robe that Grizzly Bear wears and some of the painted parfleches and shirts are based on items in the Chandler-Pohrt Collection.
The Inuit skin and hair clothing are based on items formerly in the
Chandler-Pohrt Collection and now in the Bata Shoe Museum in
Toronto.

Canadian Cataloguing in Publication Data
Lopez, Barry Holstun, 1945–
    Crow and weasel

ISBN 0-394-22176-1

I. Pohrt, Tom.   II. Title.
PZ8.2.L6Cr 1990   j813'.54   C90-094078-6

For my brother   *B. L.*

For my parents   *T. P.*

CROW and WEASEL

THE horses shivered off the night. Pintos and buckskins, sorrels and blue roans. They stood watering in the creek or continued to graze, their breath rising in steam. A few watched two young men walking out toward them from the village. As the men drew near, the horses that were dozing began to stir.

The men walked softly among them, reassuring them with quiet words, slowly separating two horses out. They eased buffalo-hair bridles over their necks and started them back to the village. The one named Weasel led, trailing a pale mare with dark brown ears. The one called Crow followed behind with deliberate calmness, walking a bald-faced pinto colt. Crow's eyes were fixed on the dark, silent doorways of the tipis ahead. Weasel stopped once, to finger blades of grass that had been cropped by an animal other than a horse in the night.

When the men had saddled their horses, they tied buckskin bags and parfleches to the saddle frames and small medicine bundles in the horses' tails and manes. They threw elkskin robes over the frames and then went to their separate lodges to say goodbye to their families. Each young man's family had opposed this trip. With the counsel of Mountain Lion, an elder who had had a powerful dream about the two men, both families had relented. But the partings, now, were not warm. What these young men proposed, their fathers still felt, was dangerous.

Crow and Weasel went alone to Mountain Lion's lodge.

"You two young men must not forget," he said, "that you are runners. You are carrying our way of life with you, for everyone to see. Listen. Be strong.

When you are tempted to give up, think of your relatives." He looked over at Weasel, sitting on his horse, and back at Crow. "Watch out for each other," he said.

Mountain Lion then gave Crow a pipe bag.

"You are not old enough, either of you," he said, "to be pipe carriers. But my dream tells me to send this with you to share with those you meet.

"Wah-hey!" said Mountain Lion, standing back. "Travel like men. Remember your people."

CROW and Weasel set out smartly, eager to be off. Mountain Lion's admonitions had made them both uncomfortable. Over the previous winter they had agreed between themselves that they wanted to travel farther north than anyone had ever gone, farther north than their people's stories went. But

their fathers had said no, it was a crazy idea, a boy's idea, and their plans had come to an end. They began talking, instead, about heading south into Aristola country to hunt for horses. Then Mountain Lion had had his dream. In the dream he saw Crow and Weasel standing on the banks of a river, the one called the Floating Ashes, the river farthest to the north in their country. In speaking about it with the other elders, Mountain Lion came to the conclusion that the two young men should revive their plans. So he convinced their fathers.

But Crow and Weasel felt their journey now bore the weight of Mountain Lion's dream. And his words to behave well and to remember their people lay heavily upon them. They forded the creek north of the village and turned to look back. It was hard to tell whether anyone returned their looks.

"We won't see this for a long time," said Crow, musing.

"Yes, but there are good signs for this trip," answered Weasel. "The grass is already good. The horses are young, strong—like us. Our mothers have made spare moccasins and given us dried meat. And I, at least, between the two of us, am a very fine hunter. What more could we ask?"

"We could ask for the blessings of the Above Ones."

"I've already done so. But you're right."

"This is not an easy thing we are trying to do," said Crow, chiding his friend. "Our fathers' counsel was good. And we shouldn't forget what Mountain Lion has said."

"I'm not afraid of what is out there, my friend. I am eager to see it."

Crow regarded his companion with pleasure. "Well then," he said. "Let's go!" And he reached over with his quirt and swatted Weasel's horse so hard on the flank the horse jumped. For a moment Weasel almost lost control. It irritated Weasel, being made to look so undignified within sight of the village.

THE two young men rode north for some days, over the shortgrass prairie. They enjoyed good weather. They crossed the Blue Mussel and the White Mussel rivers. One evening they killed a cow buffalo in country they thought the Watina belonged to, but they were not sure. Already now, the appearance of unknown flowers, especially one with tiny blue blossoms growing close to the ground, told them how far they were from their own country.

The Watina were their allies, but they understood one could never be certain about such things. So as not to be observed from a distance, they followed cutbanks and other low places in the land. Each evening they made a dry willow fire to cook, and then moved farther on, to a place where there was grass for the horses, and water. They picketed the pinto colt and hobbled the young mare and slept lightly, waking to the least sound of movement, to a distant owl call. The horses, too, frequently stood hip to shoulder, watching in both directions, restful but alert.

In the morning they ate a cold meal and went on their way, heading north by the fading stars and then the sun.

"So, do you think this country just keeps going on?" asked Weasel one morning, gazing at the unbroken horizon.

"I don't know," Crow responded.

"One time I heard someone say that the prairie ends at the edge of a forest. It was a Pityulina man. He had traveled to the other side of the Backbone of the Earth. He said there were big forests that way, and that the same forest went north of the river."

"We will see it then, if that's what he said."

"Do you think the trees will be like cottonwoods and alders," continued Weasel, "slender and all growing together, their leaves fluttering in the wind?"

"Maybe not. Perhaps they will be different."

Weasel noticed that Crow was watching the country ahead intently, and felt a little embarrassed by the way he had been carrying on, asking questions. There was plenty of time in the evening, he reminded himself, to ask questions and to talk, as the older men did when they traveled. This must be, he thought, part of what Mountain Lion had meant.

ONE day they killed a deer in a heavy willow break. Crow said they were too far north to still be in Watina country. But what lay beyond? he wondered. He turned to Weasel.

"No people with a name I know," Weasel said. "But, you know," he continued anxiously, "we've seen no signs of anyone at all. Do you think *no* people live here? There are plenty of food animals, berries, good water, grass for horses, good wood for arrows. Why would no one be living here?"

"Yes, I'm wondering too," said Crow. "You are right. We've seen no signs of horses, no signs of camps in likely places either. I think no one may live here, though it is fine country." They were both thinking the same thing but neither wanted to say it: this could be the Land of the Dead, the place where the invisible spirits of people came to live.

That afternoon, Weasel, riding far out ahead, signaled for Crow to come up quickly. When he arrived, Weasel said, "Look. We have been frightening ourselves for no reason." He pointed down at a faint trail over the grass. Crow got off his horse and examined the tracks very closely, and then nodded to his friend.

"Someone came through here, five people maybe," said Crow. "And two dogs?"

"No, three. And look how heavily everyone was loaded, look how deep the prints are. They were carrying meat back to a camp, I think, and not too far away."

"Surely you are right. We have discovered the people who have no name."

"Well," said Weasel, looking around uneasily, "let's go before they discover us."

"We might sneak up on their camp," offered Crow, "and watch them. See what they are doing."

"No," answered Weasel. "I have a feeling about this. We should just keep going."

Crow agreed and got back on his horse. "You have a good eye, to find these footprints."

"Ah!" Weasel said, waving off his words. And then, "Thank you."

THE next day they came on the river called Covered with Ashes, or Floating Ashes. It was a broad, fast, dark-water river. When they swam the horses across, Crow especially struggled. They landed far downstream on the other side. From here on, they understood, no one of their people, truly, had ever been. They dried out their things and made prayers to the Ones Above, the way they had been taught.

That evening they saw the dark line of the forest in the distance.

"From now on," said Crow as they crawled under their robes, "I think it will get more difficult." He caught his friend's eye. "Also better."

THEY had never seen anything like the forest. The trees were not at all like alders or cottonwoods, but taller, their leaves like needles, their limbs heavy, their trunks dark. And they were so close together it was hard to ride through them. Crow and Weasel had to get off and lead their horses. They were without a clear view of the sky, and being hemmed in like this made them uneasy and the horses irritable. The silence of the open prairie did not disturb them like this silence, which was oppressive and somehow threatening.

The first night they tried to sleep in the forest Weasel tossed fitfully. He began to wonder what going farther north than anyone had ever gone before really meant. Hadn't they done that, by crossing the Floating Ashes and entering the forest? How far would this forest stretch on? As far as the prairie itself, which they had been crossing for many days, for all the Moon of the Grouse Drumming?

Crow lay awake most of the night as well. He was disturbed, like his friend, about the way the dampness in the woods and the darkness were crowding them. But he was wondering, too, who the trees might be. They were beings, he knew. If your medicine was strong enough, you might be able to talk with them, ask their advice.

In the morning Weasel wondered how to raise the question of how far they were going to go, but he could sense from Crow's serious mood that he should not say anything. He kidded his friend sometimes about his failure to see the signs of animals when they were hunting, but he also knew Crow had a way of seeing that could be as powerful as his own if he learned how to use it. And he felt that that was what Crow was up to this morning, trying to feel his way through his medicine.

With extreme care, and with a nod of agreement from his companion, Crow took up the medicine pipe Mountain Lion had given them and filled the bowl. He lit the mixture of bearberry leaves and dried willow and offered it with prayers in the four directions and to the spirits above and below. Then he turned to a group of trees before him, tall and all of them looking ancient. He held the smoking pipe up to them in his two hands.

"My relatives," Crow began. "My brother and I come from far away in the south. We have never seen any beings like you. We can see that you are old and know that you must be very wise. Please, take pity on us, poor travelers far from home, and tell us who you are and what trail this is that we are on."

The silence in the woods only got deeper. Weasel, his eyes somewhat wide, looked from Crow to the trees and back to Crow.

"Have pity on us," said Crow again. "We are young men trying to understand the world. We need your wisdom."

Crow held the smoking pipe high over his head. A faint breeze stirred the needles of the trees. Weasel watched in awe as the flow of smoke rising from the pipe bowl began to reverse itself.

"You young men," began a voice that at first was almost too thin to hear, "are brave to come in here." The horses, which were tied to the trees, stamped and pivoted on their reins. "You have already traveled far," said the voice, getting stronger now and sounding more like a voice, "but you have farther to go. We are glad to help you. Sit down, and listen."

Crow and Weasel sat together before the trees, and the voice went on. "All things that are known everywhere on the earth eventually come to us, on the wind. We knew of your journey from Mountain Lion's dream, which came to us on the wind. And we know of your travels beyond the Floating Ashes River, for it has been passed along by the cottonwoods and the willows. Since our food comes to us from the earth we stand on and our longing for wisdom is satisfied by what comes to us on the wind, we never feel this need that you have to move about, to go off and discover new country. But we respect this way with you.

"The forest is dark. You will have to travel many days before you come again to country that is open. But do not be concerned. You will see a flicker. Follow her. She will show you a path. In one more moon, the Pollen Moon, you will come to a country of lakes. Our people will be very few, until there are none.

"Tell us," said the voice, "do you intend to go farther than that?"

Weasel was about to answer yes, emphatically, but he said nothing.

"Our fathers and mothers," said Crow, "with your help we will travel that far. Beyond that, we do not know. Mountain Lion only told us to watch carefully. We will look for signs and try to understand them properly. We're young. We do not know exactly how to do this. Even if we become afraid, or feel lost, we will go on, watching for a sign."

The limbs of the trees before them brushed the air, and they heard the voice again. "Yes," it said. "Be strong. Go now."

Crow and Weasel packed their few things and left. Shortly they saw a yellow-shafted flicker and began to follow her. In the morning they saw her again. It went on like that for several days, following the flashes of golden light from underneath her wings.

SUDDENLY, one day, they came upon a stranger. At first Crow and Weasel didn't know who it was, though they thought it might be Mouse. They didn't recognize the clothing at all. He was sitting on a rock on the ground with his pipe tamper in one hand and his traveling things set to one side. He didn't seem alarmed in the least by this unexpected encounter.

"We come in peace," said Weasel.

"Good!" said Mouse. "I'm a peaceful man."

"We are traveling north through these woods," said Crow.

"I am going to the west. I am on a vision quest."

"We are trying to go farther north than our people have ever gone before," offered Weasel, getting down from his mare. "Already we have come farther than anyone, but still we are going on."

"I am traveling a long way myself," said Mouse. "Among my people, west is the direction we fear most, so that is the direction we travel when we go on a vision quest."

"We have that custom among our people as well," said Crow, who had also dismounted. "Only with us, we do not travel far."

"We travel *very* far," said Mouse. "We travel to some high place and fast and wait for a dream that will give our lives a good direction."

"We have the same custom," said Weasel.

The three of them remained silent for a while.

"It's very difficult to lead a good life," said Crow, finally. "What you have set out to do," he said, turning to Mouse, "is hard. But our older people tell us that without a dream you do not know what to do with your life. So it is a good thing, I think, what you do, what your people believe."

"Yes. To be a good hunter," said Mouse, "to be a good family man, to be truthful instead of clever with people, to live in a community where there is much wisdom — that is what all of us want."

"Ah," said Crow. "But it takes your life to learn to do these things."

"Hah!" said Mouse, and they all laughed.

They camped the night together.

EVEN though the flicker led them on a path that caused no great difficulty, Crow and Weasel remained uneasy about being in the forest. The light was gloomy, and they could hear movement just beyond the reach of their eyes. Sometimes the horses snorted and shied in strange ways.

Crow had sent Mouse off that morning with a salute of his bow. Weasel had given him dried elk meat and Mouse had given Weasel a piece of stone, after showing him how to use it to make sparks for a fire. Weasel, who had been taking so long to make their fires with just a bow drill, marveled at the magic of it. Mouse's generosity, the exchange of gifts, made Weasel feel a part of something larger than himself. He felt he could carry on a long way now, no matter how dark or heavy the forest might seem.

"That was a fierce little fellow," said Crow.

"Indeed, for a small person he had great courage. Also smart. I wonder what else he had in those traveling bags."

"If he had wanted us to know, he would have told us."

"Yes," said Weasel. "I was thinking the same thing myself."

CROW'S horse stepped on a root stob in the dark one morning and came up lame. For a while Crow had to walk the narrow path on foot. It was difficult, watching the flicker and threading his way over the uneven ground. He found himself thinking how grateful he was for his horse, what a gift horses had been from the Above Ones.

That night, while they were eating, Crow said that he believed Weasel's mare, with her distinctive brown ears, was particularly good-looking.

"My father likes these brown-eared horses," said Weasel, "so we have had a few from time to time. It is difficult, though, to breed for them."

"You know that horse my uncle has with the spots—what do you call it?"

"Appaloosa."

"That's it, yes. I like that pattern in a horse. One day I would like to have a horse herd as large as my father's, nearly a hundred horses, with many of them like that. I really like that snowstorm coloring."

"You have to look for more than just the color and the pattern in a horse, though," suggested Weasel. "You have to select horses that are good close-in around buffalo, that don't frighten easily. And then you want some horses with very good feet, good night horses. And fast horses, good-winded horses, for going down into the country of the Aristola. It's nice to have the brown ears, or that Appaloosa pattern, but, as with a wife, you want a horse that's first a fine horse, not just good-looking."

"With a wife? Hah!" shouted Crow. "What do you know about it? You know nothing about women."

"Plenty! I know plenty," said Weasel.

"You know nothing. You are frightened of women. That young White Weasel Woman, the one who watched you dance, do you remember her? She made you lose your rhythm and nearly fall over."

"Yes, well, you are even worse! I think you are more afraid to talk to a woman than I am."

"That could be true, but we were talking about horses. You are the one who started talking about women."

Weasel felt annoyed, but he realized he had caused the trouble by pretending to know more than his experience had given him.

IN the middle of that night Crow whispered his friend's name. "Weasel. Are you awake?"

"Yes. Do you hear something?"

"No. I have been thinking about being in the Floating Ashes River."

"What about it?"

"When we were swimming the horses over, I felt something come up around my legs. It took hold and started to pull me under."

"What!? Why didn't you tell me?"

"I am still trying to understand it," said Crow.

"What is there to understand? You just get away from something like that—right away. You don't live in the water. A river, that's not your place."

"You have made this clearer for me," said Crow after a moment.

"What do you mean?"

"I think what it was saying to me was this: with some things in life you don't try to fight. A young man wants to fight everything, it is in him to do that. A grown man knows to leave certain things alone. Some things you don't answer. It doesn't mean you have no courage."

Weasel looked over at Crow in the dark. "My friend, were you afraid to tell me what happened back there because I would say you had no courage?"

"Something like that."

"Well, you may not always get your arrows to fly straight, and sometimes you think too much, but you are courageous, too. Take my word for it."

"It is good to be traveling together," said Crow.

"Yes," said Weasel. "And I will be happy when we are out of these woods."

AT the beginning of the Red Berry Moon—and how odd this was, they thought, for the Red Berry Moon would have already come and gone at home, far to the south; here it was just beginning, though it had been some days, really, since they had even seen the budding, prickly vines of the red berry in a forest clearing; were the moons so different here?—it was during what they thought of as the Red Berry Moon that they emerged from the trees. The air was immediately warmer, and dryer. The horses, who for so long had walked in a broken gait over the twisting, narrow path, were eager to run, to stretch out.

"Yahoo!" shouted Weasel. "Let's go!"

"Have you no manners?" said Crow, steadying his horse and scowling at his friend. Crow dismounted, gave Weasel his rein and stepped back to the forest.

"Little Sister," he cried out. "Thank you for guiding us here. Thank you for taking care of us all this way. Wherever we go we will remember your kindness. We shall wear your feathers when you give them to us. We will hold your people in regard and tell our people always to treat you well. I hope you have many children. Wah-hey!"

The flicker flew up in the air, flashing the gold beneath her wings one last time, and then flew back into the forest.

Weasel handed Crow his rein.

"It was not good of me to be thinking so much of myself," said Weasel.

"Your exuberance," said Crow, "reminds me not to take life too seriously, although here it was necessary to pay our respects. *Now* let us go. I'll race you to the top of that ridge!"

Weasel won the race, but barely. He knew, however, that his horse was slower, so he was glad.

"Let's camp here tonight," said Weasel. "I just want to stand a while in this light. I am so glad to be out of the woods."

They camped there, where the horses had good grass. They slept soundly, without the burden of heavy dreams that had been with them for so long, all of their days in the forest.

THE trees did not end abruptly but trailed out in large and small copses for several days. Finally they left the last tree behind, on a day when they could see many miles across a landscape that was like the prairie, but different. A thunderstorm was moving behind distant mountains. Crow and Weasel rode along in

a thoughtful mood. They were glad to be in open country again, even if the grasses and the flowers looked strange. The land had a deep emptiness to it that both of them could feel. They wondered if it was the empty feeling a place would have where people had never been, not a bad feeling, just new and strange.

"I've never seen country like this," said Weasel. "I am tempted to say it is like this or like that, but, truly, it is only like itself. I've been looking at these peculiar flowers, have even taken some of them out of the ground, to see how they grow, and the ground itself is different. I have seen no deer tracks, no tracks of elk or buffalo. I see the tracks of some bird that are like a grouse's track, but different. All the things here are a little different."

"I have been thinking the same thing," said Crow. "Seeing no tracks makes me uneasy. We're going to have to find something to eat soon, and the prospects are not good. I tell you, my friend," said Crow, indicating the sky with a tilt of his head, "if it were not for these last few geese and the ducks flying above us, which are familiar, I would be very worried."

"There are ducks all over these lakes, but there is no cover around the shores," agreed Weasel. "It's hard to get close enough to shoot at them. I'm worried, too. A little."

They traveled on for another day. And another. By then Weasel, too, had become seriously concerned about finding food. He was not a great hunter, but he was a good hunter, and he could find no signs of animals that he knew how to eat. That night in camp he considered telling Crow that things were not looking good for them, and that perhaps they should think about going back to the forest. Right there at its edge he had seen fresh deer tracks. But he thought to wait one more day. They could go for four or five days without food, and he was not eager to return to the forest. Besides, it would mean turning back. So he said nothing.

The next afternoon the two travelers came on a strange jumble of tracks at the edge of a lake. Weasel examined them closely, for a long while, as did Crow.

"This animal, it's something like an elk but the toes curl in further," said Weasel. "The way it stands, the way the foot spreads, I know it's an animal I have never seen. But I think it's a food animal."

"I have seen it," whispered Crow, in awe.

"What? You have never seen this animal."

"Look, there."

Weasel looked where Crow was staring. Five caribou were browsing on lichens, no farther than the reach of three arrows away, paying no attention to the two riders.

"We have to think this one out carefully," said Weasel. "Those are food animals, but they will not be easy to get to in this open country. What do you think?"

"I think we might ride straight toward them, like we do with buffalo. If they turn and run, we can chase them and shoot them."

"Maybe. But look at these lakes. We will need luck to chase them here. The ground is not good for it."

"What if you go alone," said Crow, "use my bow, hang down on the other side of your horse and approach slowly, until you are close?"

"That could work. I'll try."

Weasel mounted his horse and urged her in the direction of the caribou. He hung down on the opposite side to shield himself from sight, but the caribou hardly seemed to notice. When he got close enough, he aimed for a spot below and behind the shoulders of one animal, and shot from beneath the mare's neck. The caribou took only a few steps before sinking to its knees and keeling over. Weasel slid down off his horse. At his approach the other caribou ran.

Crow rode up swiftly. "What happened?" he asked.

"I don't think these animals have ever seen a horse. I don't think anyone has ever hunted these animals."

Crow and Weasel skinned the caribou with care, examining the meat and bones and sinews closely, and the hide. The animal had a kind of hair they had not seen before, very warm looking. And, they thought, large feet for such a creature. Its antlers were in velvet, and strange as well, neither like a moose's antlers nor an elk's but somewhere in between. Far into the evening Crow and Weasel inspected the animal, looking at the way the bones fit together, where the heart was, and at the shape and size of the lungs and the liver. They looked at the contents of the stomach. They wanted to learn the animal.

The meat was as delicious as any they'd ever eaten, though its taste was different, stronger or with a slight edge of bitterness, depending on the cut. They marveled at how tough the skin of the forelegs was, and speculated that its winter coat must be as warm as a buffalo's taken in the fall.

At the evening's end, Crow and Weasel gathered the bones and the meat they had not set out to dry and wrapped it all in the hide. This Weasel carried to a slight rise in the land, a sandy ridge close to where he'd killed the animal. He put it there and made a prayer of thanksgiving.

"Now we have plenty of meat," Weasel said when he returned. "We have the sun to guide us again. The long days of summer are here. We can keep going now."

Crow smiled to himself. He could tell that his friend had again found his desire to go on.

"Let's rest here a few days," offered Crow. "Our clothes are torn from our days in the forest, our moccasins are worn out. The horses, too, are still weak from traveling in the forest. We can repair our clothing, the horses can graze. It will be good."

Weasel agreed.

THEY spent three days repairing their shirts and leggings and making food to travel with. They dried caribou meat, and from caribou fat and some blue berries Weasel found they made pemmican. By the time they were ready to go, both of them felt refreshed, set again for a long journey. Crow had walked some miles over the country, as had Weasel; between them they now had a better sense of it. They had dug up and tasted plants — one had made Weasel violently ill — had tried to strike sparks from rocks that looked like Mouse's stone, and had set snares in which they caught large hares they didn't recognize. Weasel found a moose's tracks, a familiar animal. Overall, they felt they could survive in this country if they had to. Enough things were familiar to give them a start. The new things they could learn.

Their accomplishments put them in a good frame of mind. The morning they left they were as excited as they had been the day they left the village. Weasel, in fact, was so full of bravado that he did not notice when Crow took his knife — he lifted it deftly from the sheath and stuck it behind some bushes where Weasel had been sleeping.

"I must admit," said Weasel, "when we were going through the forest, day after day of the same difficult travel, I was getting discouraged, thinking to myself that we had really come far enough on this journey. Now I feel I could travel well into the summer before I thought about turning back."

"Is that right?" said Crow.

"Yes, I'm full of energy."

"Good," said Crow.

"Full of confidence."

"That's good."

The horses hitched and bucked lightly as they set off, glad to be traveling again. Crow and Weasel rode together and then apart for some way, and then together again, occasionally sharing a word or two about what they had seen. At one point Crow waved Weasel over, at the same time riding toward him.

"I need your knife," said Crow when they met.

"Where's yours?"

"Well, I've found something over there. I need a good knife, and yours is much better."

Weasel nodded, with some sympathy. He knew Crow was not the kind of man to carry the best implements. He was glad to help. He reached back for the haft of his knife, only to find the scabbard empty. He looked behind the saddle, thinking it might have caught on something, but it wasn't there either. He looked around now, bewildered, over the ground, and then said to Crow, "I think, possibly, my knife is not here."

"A man like you, lose his knife? Hard to believe. You must have dropped it somewhere."

"Yes, I think you're right. Let me look here a bit," said Weasel, starting back on his trail. But soon he stopped. Turning slowly around he saw Crow doubled over, convulsed in his saddle.

"What's so funny, my friend?"

"Your face," gasped Crow between bursts of laughter. "If you could see your face. The great hunter, the one all the women want for a husband, loses his knife! Hah! He looks frightened like a child!"

"I don't see what's so funny. A man who has a good knife, like me, takes these things seriously. Obviously you, an impractical man, see it differently."

"Yes, very true. You are quite right," said Crow, now more in control of himself.

"You know, I will find this knife, Crow, because I can track anything down."

"Well, I think you better start at the beginning then, because just before we left, I stuck your knife in the bushes, back there at camp."

"You did what? What?! All that distance back there!"

"It is only now that you notice?"

"You defecation of a sick calf. You cow elk!" Weasel, furious, charged. Before Crow could turn out of the way, Weasel struck him with his quirt. Crow

could not stop laughing and Weasel, suddenly feeling ridiculous, pulled up short. He, too, began to smile and to shake his head a little.

"I wish you could have seen your face," remarked Crow.

"I can't believe I spoke so foolishly," said Weasel. "A man who thinks this much of himself, surely he is one who will be distracted by the most meaningless things in life."

"I didn't hide your knife to make you feel bad, only because we were feeling so good this morning, and because I enjoy your company."

"I think you noticed how arrogant I was, leaving camp this morning, making no offering of gratitude to that place as you did. You decided I needed a lesson."

"No. I would never do that. It was only meant in fun."

"Still, you taught me a lesson," said Weasel.

"Well, I have learned many things from you on this trip. How to make a good rabbit snare. And how to stitch my moccasins so water doesn't get in. It's all the same in the end. Come on," said Crow. "We can circle back along that draw over there."

AFTER they retrieved the knife, they set off again. (This time Weasel made an offering to the Ones Above before they left.) By that evening they had ridden far into a country covered in every direction with lakes.

"It could be as hard on us here as it was in the forest," observed Weasel. "Trying to ride around these lakes is going to be like trying to ride through the trees."

"Yes," said Crow. "But it is easier to see here, and we won't go hungry."

Weasel wasn't sure about not going hungry. He had seen no more tracks of the strange animal they had killed, and he had seen no sign of moose, either. Their food might last ten days, but in country like this, where there were so few animals, it wasn't a good idea to push on. And they should be saving their dried meat, their pemmican. Who knew what lay ahead?

In camp one evening, just after Weasel struck sparks to some twisted willow bark and dry grass to cook a white-tailed hare he had shot — a terrific shot, and the only hare they had seen since trapping two near the Lost Knife Camp — Crow wondered aloud how Mouse might be getting along on his journey.

"I liked him," said Weasel, fanning the flames. "I like that kind of toughness, that courage, in anyone."

"My father is a courageous man," said Crow, reflecting. "I remember hearing stories about him from the time I was a boy, from my uncles and the other men, about his courage in the Aristola country."

"One time, you know, your father saved my father's life."

"I remember that, but tell me how it happened," said Crow.

"They were hunting buffalo, on an island in the middle of the Two Sleep River. My father wounded a big bull. The bull turned on him, threw him from his horse. He ran to the base of a cottonwood tree, where he ran around and around, unable to climb up, and that bull hooking huge pieces of bark off the tree with every thrust of his horns. My father was shouting to your father to help him, but your father didn't see him right away. When he got there my father was so exhausted he could barely move, and the bull, weakened only a little by his wound, was still after him. Your father came in hard on his horse and snatched my father up and got him away, or surely the bull would have killed him."

"It is as you say," said Crow.

"And do you know something else? That colt you are riding, his mother was dropped by the mare my father was riding that day."

When Crow glanced over, he saw the pinto staring at him.

THE maze of lakes continued. Short on food, with nothing but open country to be seen ahead and no sign whatever of people, and it being now past midsummer day, both Crow and Weasel were wondering how much farther to go. What would the sign be? Should they say this lake or that one was far enough? Indeed, had they missed something? Their eyes met nervously. Each hoped the other would speak, so they might discuss it openly.

One night in camp Crow and Weasel began to talk about their dreams. At first they were not comfortable doing so. People, they knew, needed to share their dreams if they were to learn what was in them; but it should be with the elders, who were experienced. Alone here, now, they had no other choice but to confide in each other, to try to talk out the difficult strain they were beginning to feel about the distance.

"I dreamed of that woman in the lodge next to yours," said Crow, "the one they call Crow Wing Girl. I was in a deep river, drowning. She was pulling on a long rope attached to my waist. I could feel the line tight around me, but I was stuck, I couldn't move. Then I began pulling on the line myself and I found that it worked. I pulled myself out on the shore. She was standing there with two small white buffalo calves. That was all."

28

"I can't understand this well enough to speak about it," said Weasel. "You need to tell this dream to Mountain Lion or one of the other men."

"But it is about women," objected Crow. "Maybe if we knew the women's songs, we would know what to make of this dream."

"I have been dreaming for three nights about a bear, a large brown bear," said Weasel. "We are camped somewhere, maybe in the forest, and a bear comes into camp. I am trying to get up, but the bear is standing on me. Each time it is like that, with him standing on me."

"If a bear came into a camp of ours in the forest, it would be hard to defend ourselves," said Crow.

All their dreams were heavy, but they tried to find parts in them to discuss that sounded more hopeful. They began talking to each other in a way they had never spoken before, sitting on the open tundra in the afternoon, talking about what meaning a person's life should have, what one's obligations were. They talked about how necessary it was to have experiences like the one Crow had had on the Floating Ashes. But, often, they felt they were speaking of things they didn't know much about, for they had not lived very long. And these talks shortened the time they traveled each day, which wasn't good because they did not know how far they still had to go. Still, the talks were helpful. They felt more protective toward each other, and the sense of trust between them deepened.

THE days afterward did not go well. The sameness of the land disoriented them, even after they had passed north of the maze of lakes. They were eager for a clear sign, but nothing appeared. One day Weasel's cinch broke, pitching him hard to the ground. They had to rest for a day before he could ride again. Then Crow lost his knife down a crack in a shield of rock. For half a moon they saw no food animals. Then they came on a small herd of creatures like the first one they killed, but the animals ran off. Finally, by hiding all night in some willows by a shallow lake, Crow was able to kill a moose. The meat saved them, but even this fresh food could not rid them of the feeling that they must have missed something, that they had come far enough.

The country was not really all the same. It changed subtly, and Crow and Weasel noted the differences. They were most mindful of an odd and profound change in the sky. The darkness of night was almost gone. The sun barely touched the northern horizon now before rising again. The stars had faded away. The moon was so pale they could hardly see it. They marveled at the slowness of

the light and the stillness of the earth as the sun made its transit across the northern sky.

The decision to turn back came a few days after the horses bolted camp. Something frightened them one evening. The colt pulled his picket and took off, with the mare hopping after him in her hobbles. Strangely, neither Weasel nor Crow awakened. Hours passed before they discovered the horses were missing. It was not hard to find them — the colt dragging his picket had left an unmistakable trail — but they had to run a long way before they caught up. It was clear immediately that the horses were headed south, and the significance of it came

through to each man. Still, neither said anything to the other. They rode the horses back bareback, thankful that, because the colt had waited on the hobbled mare, they had not had to chase them farther.

That evening it snowed a wet, summer snow, deep enough to cover the horses' fetlocks. Why go on? When to turn back, they knew, was a mystery not given to them to know. But they discussed it. Mountain Lion had dreamed of them coming only as far as the Floating Ashes. The Trees had seen them emerge north of the forest, and had encouraged them to look for a sign. But that was many days back, and no dream, nothing, told them of anything that might still lay

31

ahead. With the horses running away that night and their not waking up, the snowstorm — and if it was snowing already, wasn't it foolish to continue? What reason could there be to go farther?

Crow, especially, felt the weight of having to make this decision. It was he who carried the pipe, he who had leanings toward the Medicine. It was up to him, they both knew, to say, because this was no ordinary journey. As well as he could understand it, though he was reluctant to think about it directly, Crow believed he and Weasel had begun a task on behalf of all their people. No matter how difficult it became physically, nor how uncomfortable or strange, they could not turn back, not until there was a clear sign that Crow himself could comprehend.

It occurred to him that much of life was learning to wait for the right moment, and that it was a hard kind of patience to learn.

"I WILL tell you something," said Weasel one evening, after they had gone to bed. "When we started out on this trip, part of me was afraid and part of me was not. The part that was afraid had to do with Medicine things, with what Mountain Lion had said, and a little bit with the unknown, that we were going to enter a land where maybe we wouldn't know how to feed ourselves. The part of me that was not afraid was like hunger. It was a hunger to be recognized. You will not think well of me for saying it, but I do. I am not a particularly handsome man. When the girls come around from the other villages, they do not come to my lodge. And I am only a fair dancer so the others impress them more. I am a good hunter, and one day with the help of the Ones Above I may be good enough to feed a family. But, deep in my heart," said Weasel, rolling over in the dark to face Crow, "I wanted to do something no one had ever done, so the women would say of me that even if I wasn't handsome or a good dancer that I was a worthy man, a brave man, and they would consider my requests.

"I want to be right where we are now. As difficult as it has been, as frightened as we have been by these accidents and food so hard to find, I want to be here. And I want to be with you, my friend. I saw your medicine back in the forest. It is young, I know, but strong. From this time on I take the responsibility to hunt for both of us. Listen to your medicine. It makes you see what I cannot. You will now see the sign for both of us.

"I have said all I wanted to say."

Crow lay very quiet for a long time. Then he said, "My good friend, I heard everything you said. In my heart I, too, wanted to do something that would cause us to be remembered, would cause the men and women, and the young women, too, to look up to us. If that is being too proud, then it is that way. I know that you will hunt hard each day to feed us both. I will try each day, harder and harder, to understand what it is we have been given. Already this journey has taught us many things about how to be men, as Mountain Lion said it would. We are learning, too, how to watch out for each other.

"Now," said Crow, "let us sleep."

THE next morning the two men broke camp quickly and set off northward again. They did not speak at all while they rode along. Huge cumulus clouds gathered in the deep blue tower of the sky and passed away to the west. They crossed a river that was so cold Crow thought surely it came from the land where winter waits. Toward midday they stopped on a ridge that gave them a good view in all directions. Sitting there, they agreed that no people could live easily in such land. The last land for people to live in, they thought, was back near the trees.

It was unusual for them to speak much while they were traveling, for then it was too easy to miss something important. But sitting there on the ridge, Weasel felt compelled to tell Crow about a nightmare he had had a few nights before.

"We were in a strange country," began Weasel, looking out over the tundra. "It was all sandy and there were many thorn bushes and rattlesnakes like those on the prairie, and it was very hot. We were riding in a narrow canyon, one behind the other, when a strange kind of people started coming out of the rocks and attacking us. They wore some kind of gray animal skins and had loose hair, all twisted around, and long faces with small mouths and many small, sharp teeth. Their arms were long and thin, their hands, too. They had sharp nails they were raking and scratching us with.

"They wrapped their arms around our necks like ropes and pulled us down from our horses, though they were no taller than children and thin, as if they had not eaten for a long time, all the bone showing in their chests. They were biting the horses, tearing small holes that did not bleed. They tore at the horses like that until I saw the sky through them. At the same time they were tearing at us, pulling our feet off—"

"You must stop," said Crow. "Do not go any further. I had this dream last night. I know it. You describe it vividly."

33

Just then a light breeze, cold and sharp, began to flick at their clothing and at the tattered bindings of their saddles. Crow was intensely alert—he felt the thong that held a medicine bundle around his neck slip, the bundle he had made in memory of the dreams of his vision quest. He felt it sliding from his chest and he flung himself from the saddle to catch it. Crow lay still on the ground, holding the bundle up. Slowly he got to his feet. He surveyed the country ahead of them, and then looked up at Weasel.

"This place, this ridge, is the end," he said. "This is as far as we travel." He began to tie the medicine bundle back around his neck. "What lies out there is a growing darkness. We have learned what we came to learn. We have come far enough." He looked once more across the tundra, which was brilliant, sharp-edged with light. "Now we have a long way to travel before winter sets in."

Crow vaulted into his saddle and was turning his horse away when Weasel, his eyes fixed near the horizon, reached out to turn him back. Looking over his shoulder, Crow saw what Weasel was staring at. People. People in a kind of boat.

Two boats, emerging around a bend. Crow turned his horse back around and the two riders watched as the skin boats came toward them on the current of a river that gleamed black and silver in the bright sunshine.

"They have seen us," whispered Weasel.

Crow was studying the people intently. "Men and women. Dogs. Moving camp."

"I have never seen people dressed like that," said Weasel, and, he added as they came closer, "I've never seen people with faces like those. They look like Bear People."

The two boats came ahead slowly, one slightly behind the other on the river. Four people were at the oars of the first boat, their backs turned. An older man stood at the rear, facing them. There were three dogs in the boat, a kind of dog Crow and Weasel did not recognize, but not too different from dogs they knew from their home country. Also in the boat were bundles of skins, and what looked like tent poles. The rowers were watching over their shoulders and speaking to the older man.

In the boat just behind, women seemed to be at the oars, though the riders could not be sure. There was a young man at the back and three children, and perhaps some young ones moving, hidden in the skin baggage. They, too, were rowing very slowly, looking back over their shoulders at Crow and Weasel.

The boats seemed as remarkable to the two riders as Mouse's fire stone. They knew a kind of boat from their own country, made by sewing a buffalo hide around a willow frame, a round boat with one stick to guide it called a bull boat. But boats like this, made of many strange skins sewn together, with oar sticks like a loon's toes to both sides, a boat that could move so purposefully across the water, they had never seen or thought of that.

The faces Crow and Weasel could study most easily were those of the two men in the back of the boats. They seemed filled with wonder; but where the young man also seemed to be afraid, looking often to the older man for a sign, the older man, Crow saw, had another look. It was the way Weasel had looked when he was deciding to hunt the animals they had never seen before.

Just then the older man raised his hand. The people stopped rowing and backpaddled to hold their position in the slow current. By now they were only an arrow shot away. Crow raised his arm in greeting and then very deliberately made the hand sign that they came in peace, and then the sign for friend. The bearlike people did not respond, only stared.

Crow finally turned to Weasel. "Let's go down there," he said.

"Be as ready with your arrows as I will be with this lance," said Weasel.

The two riders urged their horses forward, down the slope toward the river bank. The horses snorted and yanked against their reins. Crow and Weasel felt their anxiety and each spoke calming words quietly to his horse.

The people in the boats continued to backpaddle slowly, holding their places in the current. They stared hard at the riders, but no one reached for a weapon. Crow and Weasel brought their horses to the edge of the river and stood there side by side. Weasel footed his lance in his stirrup and held its point away to show he did not intend to use it. Again Crow made the signs for peace and for friend, and then the signs for south, far, and three moon. The older man in the first boat continued to study them but he no longer revealed any emotion. The young man looked frightened. Crow and Weasel could now see clearly that they were all flat-faced people.

"I think they are afraid," whispered Weasel. "We are still on our horses. I am going to get down."

Weasel turned his lance around and stuck the point in the ground. Then he dismounted.

As soon as he got off the mare the flat-faced people gasped in terror and began to paddle backward in great confusion. The older man shouted at them to calm them, to reassure them. After a few moments of panic they gathered their composure, though Crow and Weasel could see they were still afraid. Weasel looked over at Crow. "What have we done?" he asked.

The older man, with slight inclinations of his head and quiet movements of his hands, was urging the rowers to bring the boats back downstream toward the two riders. They were almost at the same position in the river they had been before when the man said something to one of the rowers, who reached down into the bottom of the boat.

Crow and Weasel looked on in puzzlement more than fear.

Suddenly the first boat began to advance over the water toward them. A man held two huge canine teeth aloft. The boat was coming quickly. He was thrusting them toward Crow and Weasel, standing up and shouting, his long hair snapping as he did so.

Weasel's horse reared wildly, jerking Weasel off his feet and crashing into Crow's horse. The mare collapsed on her haunches and Crow's colt screamed and spun around and tried to plunge away, showing the whites of his eyes. In

truth, Crow and Weasel had never been so frightened — never had they seen teeth that large, as long as a man's arm. Whoever these people were, they thought, if they had medicine strong enough to kill an animal that big, it could only mean that they were trifling with them, drawing them in close, making fools of them first, before killing them.

Weasel, desperately trying to control his mare, had allowed her to pull him back farther from the river bank. Crow was hanging on crosswise in his saddle, but his horse had stopped bucking. He was snorting and shivering. Crow could see the people in the boat laughing. Their eyes were only slits, they were laughing so hard. When they saw Crow staring at them, hanging half off his horse, another man grabbed a canine tooth and brandished it along with the first man, who threatened Crow again by shaking the huge teeth at him.

Crow let go his saddle and dropped to the ground. To be made fools of like this, to be taunted by these people, whoever they were, made him furious. Do they think we are no one? he thought to himself, that we are so far from our home we do not know how to behave like men? Tense with fury and shaking with terror, Crow advanced deliberately toward the river bank, where Weasel's lance stood inverted in the ground. Weasel, still trying to calm his mare, patting her shuddering neck, let go the rein when he saw his friend advancing and turned for the river. The same thoughts were in his mind. If they were to die here at the hands of these people, they would die facing their enemies.

Crow pulled the lance from the ground and spun it around so that it pointed at the flat-faced people. Weasel came up alongside him with his knife in his hand. The two men stood side by side, trembling but filled with the courage of their friendship.

In that stillness the only sound was the ploink of water drops, falling from the oars onto the glassy surface of the river. The people slowly lowered their canine teeth. They looked at each other in embarrassment.

"We have killed some fine caribou," said the older man from the back of the first boat. "You young men are full of courage. The world is full of strange things impossible to understand. Let us land there where you are, and we will eat."

IT took some time for Crow and Weasel's anger to dissolve, and their fear. They stood back while the people unloaded their boats and brought them up on land, and then watched while they started to prepare a meal. A man bent over a bow drill was working vigorously to make heat for a fire. Crow and Weasel exchanged a look. Weasel walked up beside the man. Taking out the stone that Mouse had given him, Weasel struck a few sparks into the man's tinder pile. When it began to smolder the man's eyes went wide with amazement. Weasel extended his open palm with the stone, which the man took up delicately, like the leg bone of a small bird. He scrutinized it. Weasel motioned he should keep it when he offered it back. The man exhaled in disbelief. He bowed toward Weasel awkwardly, solemnly.

The older man was right. It was good meat.

"We are traveling that way," said the older man, pointing, "back to our winter homes on the ocean, hunting caribou as we go. We will stay here for a few days. We would like to have you as our guests."

"You do us an honor," said Crow. "We will stay. Perhaps you will tell us about your country. We are travelers, too, from very far away in the south, from the other side of the trees."

"The trees," said the older man with wonder. "Yes, once I heard about that, but it was too far away. None of our people have ever been there. Perhaps you will tell us, and also about the country where your winter homes are."

IN the following days the flat-faced people told Crow and Weasel many things they could hardly believe. They were a kind of people called Inuit, they said. In winter they lived at the edge of a frozen water place where, through holes in the ice, they hunted animals that looked like dogs, which they called seals. It was from an animal like that, a kind of fish-dog called a walrus, as big as a grizzly bear, that the tusks had come. When Crow and Weasel understood how tusks were different from canine teeth, they shook their heads at the way they had been fooled. The man describing the walrus laughed at the memory of the incident, at how frightened Crow and Weasel had been.

"Good one, huh?" he said.

"But why did you run from us when Weasel got off his horse?" asked Crow.

The men explained that they had never seen horses before, or any people like Crow and Weasel. "We thought at first you were two-headed animals. We were certain that, no matter what kind of animal you were, we could kill you, because there were more of us — but then you got down off that horse. We thought, this is an animal that can take itself apart! Two can become four, and then more — many more animals than our people could fight. So we were terrified."

"I see," said Weasel.

"Good one," murmured Crow to himself.

While they were talking, the man Weasel had given the fire stone to came up. He handed Weasel a knife. Its handle, made from the tusk of a walrus, was like none Weasel had ever seen. It was covered with carvings. The Inuit had told Crow and Weasel about many things they could not easily understand, about white bears that traveled over the ice and through the water and about winter lodges made from snow. About a place where the water stretched off farther than a man could travel without making camp. Too far. About a fish longer than three of the Inuit's boats and another fish with a horn in its forehead like a walrus tusk.

Weasel understood it was the winter lodges and some of these animals — the tusked fish, walruses, the white bear — that had been carved in the handle of the knife. He was speechless over the great value of this gift.

Later he offered his old knife to Crow.

ONE evening a man got up with a drum and began to tell stories. They were very like the stories Crow and Weasel had first heard as children, about the Beginning Time. Listening to them, Crow and Weasel began to long for their own people and their home country. But they were entranced by the Inuit stories — about Sedna and Tatqueq and Narssuk, about the many strange and terrible creatures the Inuit man said inhabited the land and preyed on their people. The Inuit, thought Crow and Weasel, living both on the water and on the land as they did, and living in a place where there was frost in the lodges for five or six moons each year, were a tough people and very intelligent. They were pleased to see, also, that the Inuit expressed gratitude for what they received, and that they thanked their food animals.

Crow and Weasel tried to tell some of their own stories, but they were so overwhelmed by the things the Inuit described they found it hard to speak. Crow told one or two stories about buffalo, which the Inuit understood to be a kind of heavy caribou with a big head and short horns, but more fierce than caribou. Weasel spoke about some of the good hunters, like Mountain Lion, and the Inuit marveled at that. They had never heard of that kind of animal. Crow and Weasel also told them about rattlesnakes. This animal sounded very strange to the Inuit, though they said there was a kind of people they knew, called Nakasungnaikut, who crawled around like that and killed people.

They were glad to discover that Wolf people lived among them both, and that each knew about Wolverine people.

"Of all the people," said the older Inuit man, "the Wolverine people are the toughest. In winter, when sometimes our people are starving to death, the Wolverine, they eat winter."

"We tell this story in our country, too," said Crow, "to remind ourselves of the fierceness of the Wolverine people, and to inspire ourselves in the worst times."

"We have a custom in our country," said Crow after a few moments, "to send our voices to the Ones Above. When we pray this way, we pray for all things and with everything."

The older man glanced at Crow. Something about Crow's manner seemed to please him. From under his robe, Crow reverently brought forth the pipe bag.

CROW and Weasel looked intently at everything that was presented to them during those days. They listened closely as the people explained what sort of animal each thing came from, and what it was used for. The Inuit people took them out in one of the skin boats, letting them pull the oars, and

Crow and Weasel offered the Inuit their horses to ride, though only two or three men attempted it. One tumbled off right away and was slightly injured, a scene that caused everyone, even the man who had fallen off, to laugh uproariously.

One day the older man pointed to the sun and said that it was time for them to leave, and that if Crow and Weasel wanted to get home before winter came, they too needed to go, and to travel quickly. The Inuit made caribou mittens and boots for them, and gave them tanned caribou skins and sinews and white-bear bone needles so they could keep their clothes in good repair on their journey home. The older man told them a way to go so they would pass to the east of the lake country, where the ground was harder and they could travel better.

And then they said goodbye.

CROW and Weasel traveled south for half the cycle of the moon. It was getting colder, the Moon of Dry Grass at home, but they traveled easily, riding with a confident rhythm that was new to them, which they noticed but did not remark upon. They were flush with the knowledge of all that they had learned

and seen. It would get colder and they had a long way to go. But they had covered this trail once before. And this time they were drawn on by memories of what lay at the other end.

They found caribou more easily now when they were hungry. The horses seemed more sure-footed. Both the young mare and the colt were more alert, less skittish on the path.

Under cloudless skies the horses occasionally broke away at a full gallop. Crow and Weasel rode them south with a growing sense of the wonder of what they had done.

HALF the cycle of the moon found them past the lake country, back on a path that bore their tracks. They rode for some days toward the forest. One evening before they stopped to camp they were hailed by someone in the fading light. They saw it was Badger when they rode up. She bid them enter her lodge, which was underground.

"I heard you coming toward me all day," said Badger with pleasure and excitement. "I hear everything, through the ground. Where have you come from?"

"We have been far to the north, but we live far away to the south and are headed home," said Crow.

"Well, you must stay here the night, and tell me of where you have been. There is good grass here for your horses, and no one around to bother them. We will have a good dinner and you will leave refreshed in the morning."

Crow and Weasel had never seen a lodge quite like Badger's. Quivers and parfleches, all beautifully decorated, hung from the walls, along with painted robes, birdbone breastplates, and many pieces of quillwork — leggings and moccasins, elktooth dresses, awl cases, and pipe bags. Lances decorated with strips of fur and small colored stones stood in the corners, and painted shields were hung on the walls beside medicine bundles. Other bundles were suspended from tripods.

Badger made up a good meal, and after they ate, Crow offered the pipe. In the silence that followed, Crow and Weasel felt a strange obligation to speak of what they had seen.

"Now tell me, my friends, what did you see up north? I have always wanted to know what it is like up there."

Weasel began to speak.

"My friend," said Badger. "Stand up, stand up here so you can express more fully what you have seen."

Weasel stood up, though he felt somewhat self-conscious in doing so. He began to speak about the people called Inuit and their habit of hunting an unusual white bear.

"Wait, my friend," said Badger. "Where were you when this happened?"

"We were in their camp. They told us."

"Well, tell me something about their camp."

Weasel described their camp, and then returned again to the story of hunting the bear.

"But, my friend," interrupted Badger, "tell me a little first of who these people are. What did they look like?"

Badger's words were beginning to annoy Weasel, but Crow could see what Badger was doing, and he smiled to himself. Weasel began again, but each time he would get only a little way in his story before Badger would ask for some point of clarification. Weasel was getting very irritated.

Finally Crow spoke up.

"Badger," he said, "my friend is trying very hard to tell his story. And I can see that you are only trying to help him, by teaching him to put the parts together in a good pattern, to speak with a pleasing rhythm, and to call on all the details of memory. But let us now see if he gets your meaning, for my friend is very smart."

"That is well put," said Badger, curious.

"Weasel," continued Crow, "do you remember what that man said before he began to tell us stories about Sedna and those other beings? He said, 'I have put my poem in order on the threshold of my tongue.' That's what this person Badger, who has taken us into her lodge, is saying. Pretend Badger and I are the people waiting back in our village. Speak to us with that kind of care."

Badger looked at Crow with admiration. Weasel, who had been standing uneasily before them, found his footing and his voice. He began to speak with a measured, fetching rhythm, painting a picture of the countryside where they had been, and then drawing the Inuit people and the others, the caribou, up into life, drawing them up out of the ground.

When Weasel finished, Badger nodded with gratitude, as though she had heard something profound.

"You know," she said to Weasel, "I have heard wondrous rumors of these In-

uit people, but you are the first person I've heard tell a story about them who had himself been among them. You make me marvel at the strangeness of the world. That strangeness, the intriguing life of another people, it is a crucial thing, I think, to know."

"Now Crow," said Weasel, taking his seat, "tell Badger of our people and of our village. Tell her about this journey of ours."

Crow took his place in front of the other two. He also felt awkward, but with the help of Badger, a few pointed questions to sharpen his delivery, he began to

speak strongly, with deliberation and care, about all that Weasel had asked him to say.

"You are fine young men," said Badger when Crow had finished. "I can see that. But you are beginning to sense your responsibilities, too, and the journey you have chosen is a hard one. If you keep going, one day you will be men. You will have families."

"We are very grateful for your hospitality, Badger," said Crow. "Each place we go, we learn something, and your wisdom here has helped us."

"I would ask you to remember only this one thing," said Badger. "The stories people tell have a way of taking care of them. If stories come to you, care for them. And learn to give them away where they are needed. Sometimes a person needs a story more than food to stay alive. That is why we put these stories in each other's memory. This is how people care for themselves. One day you will be good storytellers. Never forget these obligations."

No one since Mountain Lion had spoken so directly to them of their obligations, but this time Crow and Weasel were not made uncomfortable. Each could understand what Badger was talking about, and each one knew that if his life went on he would one day know fully what Badger meant. For now, all it meant was that it was good to remember and to say well what happened, if someone asked to hear.

In the morning when they left, Badger told them a way to get through the forest that was not quite so difficult as the way they had come. "It is an open trail," she said, "and there are not so many trees. You will be able to go more quickly. But, still, it is a long way to your country. And soon it will be the first Snow Moon."

She gave them each a winter robe of buffalo. They gave her a beaded bag from home, which she accepted with wonder and humility. And they said good-bye.

CROW and Weasel soon reached the edge of the forest. After only a little looking around, they found the trail that Badger had mentioned. It was wide enough for them to ride their horses on, but they decided to put off their departure. There was water and the grass was good. They would graze the horses there for a few days, and hunt caribou and dry the meat before they set off.

The last days they spent in the open were very peaceful. In the evening, in camp, they spoke of how much more confident they felt now about this country. It was, truly, a difficult country in which to make a living, but it no longer intimidated them. They could understand it, like their own country in a way. Even though there were fewer food animals and the rivers were very cold and the ground both swampier and rockier, a person could find his way here. It was not like the forest.

"Are you afraid to go back through there?" asked Crow.

"No. But I don't think it is easy, ever, even for a strong man, to be in a place where your vision is cut off and where so many of the things you hear you can't see," said Weasel.

"Yes," said Crow, "but with Badger's good advice and these warm clothes we have been given, our journey will not be so hard."

They left the next morning, their spirits still somber. The horses were frisky, nipping at each other's necks and prancing crosswise down the trail as they began.

Badger was right. The trail was good and it was easy to follow. The two riders moved at a brisk pace. It was hard to tell, because clearings in the forest were infrequent, but the gently rolling hills seemed to climb gradually to the south. Many of the creeks and the few rivers they crossed flowed away to the east. When they ran low on fresh meat they made camp and hunted, but they were unsuccessful. They caught only two rabbits in snares. Crow noticed that Weasel's winter hair was beginning to come in.

They went on. It began to snow. At first they were glad, because the snow made it easier to track animals. But there were no deer to be found, nor moose. They grew hungrier. One morning when they awoke the snow was halfway to the horses' knees. Each day they got weaker. The horses pawed relentlessly in the snow for dry grass, which was sparse. They, too, began to weaken. In some places the snow was over the horses' hocks. When the horses began to stumble from exhaustion, the two riders took turns breaking trail.

"We should have brought older horses," said Weasel one night in camp. "These horses are young like us. They are determined, but they are not seasoned, so they don't have a good rhythm. Their pace is to push and then quit instead of going steadily."

"We are doing a little better than the horses, it is true," said Crow. "In the morning let's take a robe between us and clear some of the snow away in this opening. There is bound to be a little grass. We can stay for a couple of days. One of us can watch the horses while the other hunts."

"You feel kindness for these horses, my friend. I like that."

"Think of their kindness to us," said Crow.

In the morning Weasel helped Crow clear a large patch of ground, and then he left with Crow's bow and arrows to hunt. He did not come back until after dark. Crow could tell by his silhouette as he approached that he had a deer across his shoulders.

They prepared the meat wordlessly, built up a good fire, and ate until they could not eat any more.

"I had almost given up when this one came to me," said Weasel. "I had turned back and was circling around there, only a short way off, when I saw the

movement. I notched an arrow immediately, and when I had a clear shot I took it. My arrow went wide and high. But this one did not run. Instead it took several steps toward me. I notched another arrow and shot again, but the arrow was deflected by a branch I had not seen. Still this one did not run, but stepped closer. I notched my last arrow and asked again for the Above Ones to guide it. This time it went true. He sat down, then went down on his chest. When I got to him the light was still in his eyes. I extended my hand and could feel life vibrating around him, very strong for one like this I thought. I stood away until the light faded and the eyes were quiet."

"Well, the Above Ones heard you, perhaps even before you asked for their help."

"I never forget now to give thanks, to them, to this one. In the morning we must put these bones in a tree, where no harm will come to them."

They slept well. They felt strong. When they awoke during the night they heard only the horses grazing on dry grass, their hooves chirping on the cold snow.

They let the horses graze another day. Then they departed.

FOR more than half the cycle of the moon they traveled through the forest, finally coming to its edge. Food was still hard to come by, and the riders and their horses were again both weak. But they were out of the forest now and back in country they knew far better. Weasel was confident that here, where the snow was not so deep and where they were likely to find both elk and buffalo, they would soon find food.

"We are still north of the Floating Ashes," said Crow. "The river must be much farther to the south here, for we have already traveled a day and there is no sign of it ahead. We will both have to be alert."

"Let's camp down there in that swale," said Weasel. "We can strip cotton-wood bark to feed the horses. Tomorrow, each of us can range out, one east, one west, to look for tracks. I am sure we will find something. We will kill a buffalo."

Weasel's words disturbed Crow profoundly. It was not good to speak with such confidence about hunting, he thought. Hunting was difficult, always, even when it looked easy. You couldn't find animals if they didn't want you to. If any animals had been listening, surely now they had left the country.

The next day Crow and Weasel fanned out to the east and the west, but they did not find any animals. They traveled on, another half-day's journey, and fed the horses once more on the bark of cottonwood trees. The following morning they walked out again, hunting without success. Two more days it went like this. Crow and Weasel hardly had strength enough to move around. They were lying still under their robes that night, trying to sleep, when Weasel said, "This is my fault. Back there, I should never have said with such arrogance that we would find what we were looking for. I think the animals heard me and now they have gone away."

"Perhaps."

"I have been trying to see what I should do. I must humble myself before the Above Ones and ask for their pity."

With these words Weasel rose from his sleeping place and began to undress. He took off his robe and his shirt, then his leggings and the rabbitskin socks he had made and the fur boots the Inuit had given him and stood naked in the snow. In the moonlight Crow could see that his hair was now almost completely white.

Weasel walked off across the prairie to a place where no one could see him, and there he went down on his knees and raised his arms over his head.

"The Ones Who Live Above, hear me. My relatives, hear me. My heart is sad over this terrible thing I have done. Have pity on me. I am here before you without my clothes, the protection against the cold that the animals have given me. I beg you to hear my prayer, to accept my expression of humility and sorrow. I promise you that I will never again act as though I expected the land to feed me. I will remind myself, always, that this is a gift, to be fed and clothed and protected from the weather by the animals is a gift. I will remember it. And I will always return something to the animals, as long as I live. Please hear my prayer. My relatives, please, help me. Ones Living Above, see the sorrow in my heart."

He remained there on his knees, still as the moon in the cold silence.

WHEN Weasel came back into camp, he was struggling so hard against the cold Crow had to help him get his clothes on. He helped him to the ground and covered him with his robe.

They both slept.

In the morning they were too weak to move. During the day Crow rose to melt water for them. He had to hold Weasel's head so he could drink.

"I think now," said Weasel, his voice a shadow torn by sadness, "there is only one thing to do. We must kill one of the horses. If we do not, we will die here."

Crow did not respond to the words, but he knew his friend was right. The horses stood near the bare trunks of the cottonwood trees he had stripped for them. Crow felt dizzy with hunger. It was hard now to make any sense of the country. He thought they must have gotten turned around, for the forest was now, again, quite close to them. In his heart he spoke prayers of his own to the Ones Above, but he knew this was Weasel's affair, that it was not his business. He looked once more at the colt and the mare. He did not want to think what it would be like. One part of him could kill easily, because they were starving. But another

part of him had no wish to take life, and he recognized in this one of the great problems of living, which before had never been so apparent to him.

He went to bed without meeting the horses' eyes. "In the morning," he said to Weasel.

THEY did not awaken until late, and when they did they saw someone standing there in camp. It was Grizzly Bear.

"My friends," said Grizzly Bear softly, "you are very weak. Do not try to move. I have brought some elk meat for you. Rest there, while I build up the fire."

Grizzly Bear prepared the meat over the fire and served them where they lay. The two men ate in silence, so weak their eyes were rolling back in their heads. They nodded toward Grizzly Bear, to let him know their gratitude. After they had eaten a little they fell asleep. Crow tried to speak, but Grizzly Bear told him to sleep for a while.

When they awoke again, Grizzly Bear was there tending to the fire. "Would you like some water?" he asked. He gave them water in a buffalo horn cup. They drank it, and then he gave them more meat.

"You have saved our lives," said Crow. "Our gratitude is very deep."

"I saw you from a distance. I could tell by your stillness you were starving," said Grizzly Bear.

It was evening. The sun had gone under some clouds that were golden and white. Grizzly Bear raised his eyes to look at the sunset, and then told a story. He was traveling in this country once, all alone, he said, and he was starving. It had been a long moon since he had eaten. He was so weak he was barely able to walk. One evening, very much like this one, he said, he was lying in a draw and he saw a flock of geese fly across the face of the sun.

"It was only a moment," said Grizzly Bear, "but it was so beautiful it went straight into my heart. I got up and went on. In the last light that day I found what I was looking for. With my last strength I accepted the life of that animal. I ate and then I slept. I ate and slept again, and then I was able to go on."

"Sometimes it is what is beautiful that carries you," said Weasel weakly from his bed.

"Yes. It can carry you to the end. It is your relationship to what is beautiful, not the beautiful thing by itself, that carries you," said Grizzly Bear.

The clouds hanging before the sun had turned indigo underneath and were glowing a soft rose above. The light fell differently on each one of them. The side of Crow's head gleamed like obsidian. Weasel's fur glowed like freshly fallen snow. Grizzly Bear's coat glimmered like water, a dazzling mixture of gold and red, of yellow and brown and silver light. The eyes of each one, despite the weakness of the two riders, seemed as if lit from within.

"Sleep, my friends," said Grizzly Bear. "When you awaken in the morning, you will be strong enough to travel. I will feed your horses before I go. Remember me."

"Wah-hey," said Weasel faintly. "Holiness."

"My friend!" Crow cried out. "Wait! What can we give you?"

"You can give me nothing, Crow. I feel your gratitude. That is enough." Grizzly Bear paused. Then he said, "Be kind."

"May you travel safely, my brother."

"Wah-hey," said Grizzly Bear, and he was gone.

A FEW days later Crow and Weasel came to the banks of the Floating Ashes. The river had frozen over. It had been snowing since they left the Grizzly Bear camp and, though they were much stronger now, the cold came down hard on them. Their feet and hands were stiff and the riding was difficult. But from

here, they knew, it was not more than half the cycle of the moon to their own country. It only remained to cross the river.

Weasel went first, after searching in several places for where the current would be slowest, the ice thickest. He was part way across when Crow started over. Just a little way out from shore Crow heard ice cracking beneath his horse. He started to get down, to spread the weight, but before he could the horse broke through. Dark water boiled up around both of them. Weasel heard Crow's shouts and turned quickly to see what had happened. As he watched he saw the current dragging his friend underneath the ice, the horse, flailing wildly, struggling toward shore. Weasel jumped down and ran back. He grabbed hold of Crow but the current was terrific. He could not get any footing strong enough to pull him out. The colt was lunging desperately, cutting his belly on the ice and showering the snow with his blood.

With one hand Weasel held tenaciously to Crow. With the other he chopped furiously at the ice, until he had cut a cleft to hold Crow against the current. He could see by Crow's eyes that the cold was beginning to take his spirit.

"Hold on, my friend! Hold on!" shouted Weasel, running for the shore. He grabbed Crow's horse by his head to steady him and the pinto finally plunged ashore through the broken ice. Weasel pulled his picket rope free and stripped him of his saddle. Leading him by the rein, talking gently, he brought him quickly back out onto the ice, downstream from Crow, whose eyes were now barely open. Weasel tied the latigo from Crow's saddle around Crow's shoulders and then tied him to the horse with the picket rope. With the colt pulling steadily and Weasel reaching under the ice to swing Crow free of the current, they got him out on the snow. Weasel pulled off Crow's clothes and wrapped him tightly in his own robe. He then ran to the other shore.

From his bag Weasel took his firemaking equipment, and for the first time briefly regretted having given Mouse's fire stone away. But soon he had a little tinder burning, which he fed with dry sticks. When the fire began to blaze he went back to Crow, who was barely conscious. Weasel pulled him across the snow to the fire, where he wrapped him in a dry sleeping robe. Then he went to look after Crow's horse.

They camped there that night. Weasel broke all the ice out of Crow's clothes. By morning, everything was dry.

"This river," said Crow as they saddled the horses. "I will not try to cross it again."

SOME days later they saw smoke on the horizon. The following day they came over a rise and recognized in a valley below the lodges and the horses of their people.

"It's too bad we do not have really good-looking clothes to wear now," said Weasel. "Fancy bead and quillwork, lots of tassels, moose-hair embroidery. It would be a very proud way to return." He meant for Crow to smile, but he didn't.

"I think we look good," said Crow, "And we are alive."

They regarded each other for a long moment and then they descended into the valley.

WHEN they drew near the camp no one saw them at first. It was the horses who alerted those in their lodges, the whinnying of the horses in the herd and the nickering of the two horses approaching, those calls flying across the hills. Slowly, then more quickly, by twos and threes, people emerged from their lodges. When the two riders got off their horses they silently embraced their fathers and mothers, their grandparents, their brothers and sisters.

Mountain Lion and the others came up quietly in the snow.

"We have traveled a long way," said Crow, looking at Mountain Lion. "We went where we said we would go. We smoked the pipe with the people who live in that far place. They send their greetings. They heard our stories, and they convey their respect. We saw many wonderful things. In time, we will speak of it."

Crow then held out the pipe bag for Mountain Lion to receive. Mountain Lion took in the details of their clothes, their saddles, the condition of their horses. He studied the riders' faces. "That is your pipe now," said Mountain Lion to Crow. "You are a pipe carrier." The horses stamped impatiently. "We are proud of both of you."

Turning to Weasel, Mountain Lion waited for him to speak.

"Crow has put it well," said Weasel. "In time, when we have been with our families and walked in these snowy hills, we will tell the stories that were given to us. We will share all we have learned."

"In a few days," announced Mountain Lion, "we will have a transferring ceremony. In the future, our traveling bundle will hang before Weasel's lodge."

There were expressions of disbelief among some of the people at this pronouncement. "Mountain Lion," said Red Fox, speaking for several of them, "these are young men. No young men like this have ever carried the pipe, or guarded the traveling bundle."

"It is clear to anyone who can look who these men are," said Mountain Lion. "Their years are not many, but they have made a great journey. It is a journey we will talk about for many winters to come. The wisdom they have brought home is now our wisdom. This pipe and this bundle are in the right hands."

Everyone nodded agreement in the face of Mountain Lion's words. Red Fox reached out and touched the young men's shoulders.

AT first, Crow and Weasel said little about what had happened to them, following the custom of their people. They were brought back into the flow of events in the village, to hunting and winter tasks in the lodges. They alluded, almost teasingly, however, unable always to control themselves, to such things as the Inuit's boats and to Mouse's fire stone. And people took up and examined their caribou-skin clothes and marveled at Weasel's Inuit knife.

Late one afternoon, the day Mountain Lion had appointed for people to gather in his lodge to begin to hear the stories of their journey, Crow and Weasel were walking on the western edge of the village. They were speaking of what the

things they had done meant to them, and of how the stories should go, and, as the sun began to set, they were watching the horses.

"Look, over there," said Weasel, pointing with his chin. "Look how the others follow our horses around."

"Yes," answered Crow. After a while he said, "I wonder if, in the future, people will continue to travel like this?"

"I will urge my children to do what I have done," said Weasel. "Whether they are young men or young women, I will urge them to go."

"That is new thinking for you," said Crow.

"Our journey, seeing different ways of life, has made me wonder about many things," said Weasel. They stood in silence together, their breath rising in a fog.

"One day perhaps my son will travel with your son," said Weasel. "They will return and the people will listen to what they have to say. And then their children. It will go on like that, and that way our people will look into the heart of wisdom."

Crow pondered his friend's words. His eyes followed an Appaloosa mare on the hill below them. "The wonder and the strangeness," he said, "the terror of the world, will never be over." He turned and regarded Weasel. "Imagine our daughters," he said. "Traveling."

The noise of someone moving firewood in camp drew their attention away for a moment.

They drew their robes closely around them. "Look at the sun," said Weasel. The clouds that stood before the sun had taken on a soft, yellow tinge. Far out to either side the sky was lit with wisps of cloud glowing red and orange, ribbons of burning winter light, trailing off into pale salmon.

"I wonder if in the country where Grizzly Bear lives the sun is setting like this," said Crow. "I hope it is. I hope as we speak that this light, this color, is streaming down on him."

In the silence that followed, Weasel said very softly, "It is good to be alive. To have friends, to have a family, to have children, to live in a particular place. These relationships are sacred."

"Yes," said Crow. "Yes, this is the way it should be."

And they turned and began walking up through the snow together toward Mountain Lion's lodge.

Design by David Bullen
Typeset in Mergenthaler Cochin
by Wilsted & Taylor
Printed by Dai Nippon Printing Company